THIS BOOK BELONGS TO:

Other Kipper Books

Kipper
Kipper and Roly
Kipper's A to Z: An Alphabet Adventure
Kipper's Birthday
Kipper's Christmas Eve
Kipper's Toybox
Kipper's Snowy Day
Where, Oh Where, Is Kipper's Bear?
Kipper's Book of Colors
Kipper's Book of Numbers
Kipper's Book of Opposites
Kipper's Book of Weather
Kipper's Rainy Day (Lift the Flap)
Kipper's Sunny Day (Lift the Flap)
Kipper Has a Party (Sticker Story)
Kipper in the Snow (Sticker Story)
Kipper and the Egg (Touch and Feel)
Kipper's Sticky Paws (Touch and Feel)

Little Kippers

Arnold
Butterfly
Hissss!
Honk!
Meow!
Picnic

Rocket
Sandcastle
Splosh!
Swing!
Thing!

Skates

Mick Inkpen

Red Wagon Books
Harcourt, Inc.
San Diego   New York   London

Tiger had some brand-new skates.

"They're Rollerblades," said Tiger. "Much better than ordinary skates, Kipper. Look, the wheels are all in a line!"

Tiger was not very good
on his new skates. He
kept wobbling and falling.
   Then he rolled off down
the slope, waving his arms
and shouting, "Get out of
the way!"

He crashed into Pig, who was walking with Arnold in the park.

Tiger struggled to his feet, and then fell over again.

"I haven't got any skates," said Pig. "Can I try yours?"

"No," said Tiger. "No, I wouldn't want you to hurt yourself. No."

So Kipper let Pig try his skates instead.

Pig was a terrible skater. He couldn't even stand up!

"What you need is practice," said Tiger. He was so busy telling Pig how to do it, he didn't notice he was rolling down the slope again.

He crashed into a bush.

"Ow!" shouted Tiger. He had hurt his thumb. "Ow! Ow! Ow!" He wasn't very brave.

Kipper took him home for a Band-Aid. Tiger wanted some ointment, a sling, and some candy, too!

"Let's go and show Pig my bandage!" he said.

When they arrived at
Pig's house, Pig and
Arnold were in the garden.
Pig was still wearing
Kipper's skates.

"I want to show you
something!" said Pig. He put
on some music and began
to skate.

"Wow!" said Kipper and
Tiger together.
Pig had been practicing.
He was brilliant!

And Arnold wasn't bad, either.

www.harcourt.com

Illustrated by Stuart Trotter

Library of Congress Cataloging-in-Publication Data
Inkpen, Mick.
Skates/Mick Inkpen.
p.   cm.—(Little Kippers)
"Red Wagon Books."
Summary: Even with his new in-line skates Tiger is a terrible skater,
but Kipper is good and, with a little practice, so is Pig.
[1. In-line skating—Fiction.   2. Roller skating—Fiction.   3. Animals—Fiction.]   I. Title.
PZ7.I564Sk   2001
[E]—dc21   2001002057
ISBN 0-15-216247-X
A C E G H F D B
Printed in Hong Kong

DEMCO